ANNAM

For Debby. Christmas 1996.

Love,

Mary

CHRISTOPHE BATAILLE

ANNAM

TRANSLATED BY
RICHARD HOWARD

A NEW DIRECTIONS BOOK

Note: The 18th-century spellings—Viêt-nam, Viêt-namese—are used throughout the text.

Book design by Sylvia Frezzolini Severance
Manufactured in the United States of America
New Directions Books are printed on acid-free paper.
First published clothbound by New Directions in 1996
Published simultaneously in Canada by Penguin Canada Limited

Library of Congress Cataloging-in-Publication Data
Bataille, Christophe.
  [Annam. English]
  Annam / Christophe Bataille : translated by Richard Howard.
    p.   cm.
  Translated from French.
  ISBN 0–8112–1330–7 (clothbound)
  I. Howard, Richard, 1929–   . II. Title.
PQ2662.A842A8413   1996   96–24528
843'.914—dc20   CIP

Celebrating 60 years of publishing for James Laughlin
by New Directions Publishing Corporation
80 Eighth Avenue, New York 10011

SPEAK WITH GOD ONLY
OR ONLY OF GOD.
—St. Dominic

ANNAM

CHAPTER I

When the Emperor of Viêt-nam arrived at the French court in 1787, Louis XVI's reign was foundering in gloom. The King was ageing; criticisms were snide. The Queen had forsaken him, his councillors were impatient: agitation beset the realm. The very panels of the Château of Versailles were flaking: tiny gold flowers ready for an autumn capitulation.

Vast stretches of the park lay fallow, magnificently so: yellow, ochre, red. One could stroll here long hours in solitude. Aside from the Great Lawn, only the Grand Canal and the fountains remained splendid. For water still had to be piped through them on the occasion of the *Fêtes du Soleil*.

The Emperor of Viêt-nam was only seven years old, his name was Canh. He had reached Brest after nine months at sea. Peasants in the northern provinces of his country had rebelled and driven their Emperor from his palace at Hué. His father deposed, the Prince Regent, Nguyen Anh, had sought refuge in Siam. Alone, he was helpless; but he knew that on the other side of the world there was a country as rich as it was kind, and powerful in war: France. He had been told of Louis XVI's ancient power and the glories of his kingdom. He dispatched his son to the reigning king. Nguyen Anh wanted his throne; he invited France to send troops and missionaries to establish by force the Kingdom of God.

Canh knew some French words. He was an odd little boy, delicate, tormented by loneliness, abandoned to a new kind of solitude. He was discovering a world apparently benign; his flat countenance and his features attracted attention. He was regarded with respect and a certain interest. His arrival at the château was greeted by bored courtiers hungry for novelty.

Everyone had his own dreams of Viêt-nam. Strange rumors were rife concerning its fauna; its flora too was apparently inhuman: giant trees, monstrous flowers. The subject was suddenly fashionable—utterly unknown and on everyone's lips. One evening, as the King was dining in silence, it occurred to the Duc de Châtelet to speak of Viêt-nam; Louis XVI listened patiently, then interrupted: "Monsieur, that will do; our kingdom is already great; it will remain so, if God permits. Let our foolish ambitions go no further."

Little Canh was surprised by how cold the autumn was; in his country he knew nothing of the trees' mournful colors. The park of Versailles was gloomy. Yet it was here that the Emperor met the courtiers' children; oblivious of his solitude, they invented cruel tricks to play on him. Then Canh would shed his tears, consoled by the ladies-in-waiting; they brought him to their mistresses' apartments where he was a little animal, a new toy.

One day, as he was wandering through the great corridors of the South Wing, Canh glimpsed a tall dark shape ahead of him: he ran toward it, for he thought he had recognized a mask from his own country. During the Feasts of Têt it was the custom to imitate death in order to banish it. Canh stopped a few steps from Bishop Pierre Pigneau de Bréhaine who, wearied of his Bishopric of Adran, was retiring from the world. About to be received by the King, he was meditating in solitude. "Good evening, my son," he said. He hesitated: was this the Emperor of Viêt-nam? Pierre Pigneau de Bréhaine did not know. He made a swift decision: "Come, my son; let us pray for your country and your father."

Little Canh was glad to be listened to, at last. He took the hand of the tall dark shape, and the two of them entered the chapel of Versailles. Only the Bishop prayed, kneeling on the Parma velvet. Canh ran about the chapel, dazzled by the candles of gold leaf, dismayed by the silence. He chattered away in his language; Pierre Pigneau de Bréhaine smiled amid his prayers. He loved this child but found him far from his own kind, and far from God.

At last Canh was presented to the King. The Emperor entered the Throne Room; Canh offered Louis XVI a parchment discolored by the sea air, bearing the seal of Viêt-nam. In it, his father presented his appeal.

Slowly, the King read the text. He sighed, gazing at the child. Each was bored to a like degree. Louis XVI set aside protocol and said: "My child, our kingdom no longer enjoys its former wealth. Your country is distant, mine in distress. Your people suffer, but the people of France affect me more closely."

A murmur ran through the crowd of ministers: was this the grandeur of the kingdom of France? Louis XVI raised one hand and concluded: "Come to us if you so desire; but France will not go to Viêt-nam."

The King indicated that the interview was at an end. Canh had not understood its true purpose. He wanted most of all to get out of his laces and stockings, which were stifling; women with sweet smiles were waiting for him, and the tall shadow with fatherly eyes.

Pierre Pigneau de Bréhaine taught the young Emperor the first words of his catechism; the Bishop had surprised Canh in a nursemaid's arms. The child had been crying, he was lonely. She had consoled him; he was sucking her breast heavy with warm milk. The Bishop wrested him from the sins of woman. He taught him these words: "My Lord, I am very sorry to have offended Thee, for Thou art infinitely good, and sin is hateful to Thee. I solemnly swear, with the help of Thy Grace, never to offend Thee more and to do penance."

With difficulty Canh repeated the words and

stared timidly at the black shadow with blue-gray eyes.

Several days later, the young Emperor of Viêt-nam died of pneumonia. The court filed in silence past the little body with its strangely bluish countenance. Death was commonplace, solitude less so. French children died within their family. Canh had left behind his country, his own people; he had wandered, alone, in the vast apartments of the château. Doubtless he had not been able to sleep. They found him one morning in the Hall of Mirrors, dressed in a simple cotton gown, barely lit by the rising sun.

How far away Viêt-nam was!

There had been no news of Prince Nguyen Anh; having taken refuge in Siam with his partisans, he was preparing his revenge, waiting in vain for a sign from the Kingdom of France.

Louis XVI, however, was moved by the Emperor's death; he offered him a Christian burial in the little cemetery, behind the château.

Pierre Pigneau de Bréhaine insisted that these words be written on his tomb:

For my God and for my country

The Emperor of Viêt-nam had died a Catholic.

CHAPTER II

Time had passed.

The former Bishop of Adran was weary of his retreat at Saint-Benoît-sur-Loire. He meditated as he stared at the plains, brown in autumn, white in winter. All day he walked beside the Loire, benumbed by the cold. Under the old stones of the abbey he offered God the soldier's prayer: "Lord God who loves us, help us to be strong."

France had always been the Church's eldest daughter. Pierre Pigneau de Bréhaine was profoundly good; he had loved Canh with all the severity of his heart. As a man of faith he loathed those fatuous abbés who delighted in flesh, in gold. He reflected often upon Viêt-nam at war, forgotten by all. Bur God forgets no one.

On December 27 of the year 1787, two months after he had entered the abbey, Pierre Pigneau de Bréhaine left his retreat. An ultimate task lay before him. He obtained audiences with influential men. Rich benefactors, concerned with their salvation, came to his aid; others sought to wrest Viêt-nam from impiety. The fashion for such things had passed, like the wind, like the age, but the old Bishop managed to collect one hundred and fifty thousand gold écus. He armed two huge ships, the *Saint-Jean* and the *Saint-Paul:* John was Christ's beloved apostle, Paul had made converts beyond the sea.

On April 4 of the year 1788, the harbor of La Rochelle was noisy with rumors, and with men bearing heavy burdens. A pale sun caressed bright-colored bundles, dried beef, gunpowder. Men bearing arms embarked with joy, as though for a crusade. They were strong, proud. A group of Dominican monks were praying together, as well as five nuns.

"Lord, help us to protect Thee, to make Thee known, to make Thee loved. Let us pray for those we are about to help."

The crowd watched all this agitation. These people were leaving for the ends of the earth; Viêt-nam was unknown. The *Saint-Paul* and the *Saint-Jean* were getting under way with their missionaries and their soldiers-in-arms. The voyage would last several months: sacks were stowed—dried fruit, cherrywood crucifixes; rigging furrowed the decks. Everything awaited the coming of Pierre Pigneau de Bréhaine.

Louis XVI did not favor the expedition. But it was supported by the Church: Canh had not been forgotten.

At the last moment, Brother Dominic came aboard: he had returned from the Americas. The Kingdom of God would never be great enough; the monk therefore offered himself to the former Bishop of Adran, and embarked for Viêt-nam.

On the morning of April 19 of the same year, Pierre Pigneau de Bréhaine stood on the quays of the long harbor of La Rochelle. He felt close to death and wished to remain with his own people. In the presence of the citizens, he blessed the two ships and offered chaplets from Jerusalem to the missionaries, rosaries to the nuns.

"God keep you, my children!"

The ships left the harbor just after dawn.

CHAPTER III

The two ships put into port at Morocco. They had endured a long storm off Portugal: torn sails had to be mended, the rudder straightened, a sick sailor put ashore. On the third day of the voyage, rats were discovered in the hold; a portion of the dried beef had to be burnt. Incessant disasters afflicted the ships. At Tangier, all could rest in the shade of the palms. The sea was splendid, reflecting the blue winds to infinity.

They remained in Tangier for several days. And it was time to set out again. A strange languor overcame the crew. The soldiers were uneasy: Viêt-nam was unknown. They often imagined, in long conversations, a monstrous vegetation: the rains were said to be terrible, the ferns inconceivable, always green, the animals terrifying. By the light of a full moon, strong men visibly trembled. Cockroaches infested the ship; small ones. What would they be like on the other side of the world?

The *Saint-Jean* and the *Saint-Paul* followed the African coast. The blue, then ochre, deserts close to the horizon had disappeared. In the southern part of the continent, landscapes were gray, studded with mountains. The sky was occasionally lacerated by white storms. They were approaching the Cape of Good Hope; it was sighted the summer of the year 1788.

Two months had passed since landing at Tangier. They put in not far from the Cape. Sister Jeanne discovered strange flowers, red, orange or blue, whose pistils constituted a sort of natural wool. But the Cape was ravaged by cholera. The city was sealed to the world: they could not anchor here.

From a privateer they learned that Pierre Pigneau de Bréhaine had died, among his family, on his estates at Vouvray. Hence he would never know the consequences of his expedition; he would never know Viêt-nam. For all of them, he remained the man who had raised his hand and wept, one morning, in the harbor of La Rochelle. But his great work must continue.

The ships set sail and doubled the Cape of Africa.

They coasted Madagascar; the island was lovely, blue and green between sea and sky. The crew daydreamed, imagining France, but also these new lands.

One of the sailors died of scurvy; his teeth were black, and fell out. The missionaries prayed a long time, while the nuns sliced limes. For several weeks the voyage was punctuated by this continuous sucking which saved the crew from sickness.

When the *Saint-Jean* and the *Saint-Paul* sailed north toward the mysterious Indies, the nights grew shorter. The sky darkened to a velvety black, and a quartermaster discovered new stars. The elements were indistinct now: night was a long dream. In the cool of the evening, the sailors stretched out on deck between the coils of rigging and dreamed, resting their heads on their hands. The universe seemed to expand. For several days the wind fell. They took advantage of the calm to mend the *Saint-Paul*'s mainsail.

The deck became scorching. The missionaries had abandoned their soutanes; they were dressed like the sailors now. The nuns began to grow accustomed to this strenuous life: the oaths of the crew, the sweating bodies, the wormy water and sour wine of the casks. The extreme humidity penetrated every item of clothing and imbued each object, each person, with an inescapable clamminess.

The captain was a born story-teller. He had sailed all over the world and knew Brother

Dominic well. They had set out together for the Americas. One sultry night when no one could sleep, the captain told them of far-off Québec; there summers were ochre and mournful, and deep blue lakes dotted the mountains. You could swim in them, your body conscious of the depths beneath. These ever-different worlds made them forget the rats running beneath the deck, the ships' ponderous sleep. The captain also knew tales of the East; they were peaceful, beautiful. Viêt-nam suddenly seemed closer.

Then the wind rose again.

At the end of October, the nights grew longer, and pale. In their sleep the men would huddle together to keep from shivering.

Seven months had passed; the ships' names had almost disappeared. Every inch of the white sails was patched. Stores were exhausted; they had to be satisfied with sun-dried salt fish. Men began falling sick. One missionary died, and two sailors. Their sufferings were terrible.

One morning, Ceylon was sighted. They put into port for two weeks. The sailors discovered the brothels; they lingered there a long while, fascinated by the gold hangings and the dark-velvet women. The Dominicans and the nuns visited the town. Everything was different. From so far away, France had become unreal. They did not know that the peasants of their country were in revolt; that the nobility was anxious. Sometimes it occurred to Louis XVI to dream of the distant countries which seemed so calm to him; he would imagine impenetrable forests, a swarming pygmy populace, their languages strange.

The banners were struck; finally the sails were changed. New provisions were bought with the Church's gold; the names of the ships were repainted, blue. Viêt-nam must be entered in the glory of the Kingdom of France. A huge crowd came to see off these strange travelers, these austere and sometimes lovely women. The nuns had abandoned their dark coifs: their hair was blond, more often than not, and long: a wonder to the inhabitants of Ceylon.

The moorings were cast off. The next port would be the city of Saigon, in the Mekong delta.

France maintained embassies and commercial banks around the world. So the expedition's progress was known at Versailles. The wildest rumors spread. Terrible diseases broke out, in those regions; the Church was squandering its gold to no purpose; this was one of the king's follies. Nonetheless, Viêt-nam returned to fashion; in conversations at court, the courtiers were ecstatic. The people were exhausted by useless conquests. Then everyone forgot about these two ships, lost in the tremendous distance. The peasants were hungry, the Jacqueries multiplied.

Christmas of the year 1788 was celebrated on board the *Saint-Jean*. A midnight Mass was said; the wind was mild. The sails were lowered so that enormous torches could be lit. The sailors knelt and prayed. The sky was pale, the sea infinite. There was no holiday meal, for there were no fresh supplies. As usual, they had to be satisfied with dried fruit and limes. The captain offered a round of rum; no one refused, not even the long-haired nuns. France seemed so far away, suddenly, and Christmas not so gay as they had hoped. Brother Dominic began murmuring a Vendéan song; one sister wept. Drunk, the captain talked all night long, describing Mexico, its strange pyramids, the scorpions, the red desert. By morning, the wind had risen.

The voyage seemed to be approaching its end. But everything fluctuated: They had to drop anchor off unknown, beautiful lands. An archipelago with bitter palms. The sea was bright and disturbing somehow, lined with sharp pink corals. Sister Armande was suffering from an unquenchable thirst. Under the heavy linen bedclothes, she shivered. Her face quickly grew thin, then skeletal: it was cholera. The *Saint-Jean* was evacuated. The captain wanted to burn the vessel and abandon the wretched woman, for whom nothing could be done. Brother Dominic strenuously refused and remained, with Sister Armande, shut up in the hold of the *Saint-Jean*. Her agony lasted twelve days. On the other ship, everyone prayed, not knowing what else to do; were the two missionaries dead? By night, the torch-flames were reflected in the sea, and there was silence. On the morning of the thirteenth day, Brother Dominic emerged from the hold, a heavy sack on his shoulders. He was exhausted, but calm. He burned Sister Armande's body, then did the same for whatever he found on board: provisions, rigging, sails. Only the gunpowder and the cannons remained. The crewmen, gathered on the *Saint-Paul*, watched Brother Dominic shave. He dived into the sea and swam the whole morning.

France believed both ships lost, cargoes and all hands. A Mass was said in the Chapelle Royale for those who had engaged in the expedition. This was the first time Viêt-nam was forgotten.

The helmsman was the first to notice the green stripes silhouetted against the horizon. Since January, the heat had grown more intense. It was in May that Viêt-nam appeared. Everyone was relieved. The men were bearded now; the nuns had made themselves light gowns—like the dresses of peasant girls in the south of France. They could discern the rice-fields, a brilliant green, and human silhouettes bending over the earth.

The voyage was beginning.

CHAPTER IV

The captains decided to anchor offshore at Saigon. The sailors stayed on deck, in the starry night, speculating about the country of which they had dreamed.

In the morning, a fruitless search was made for the nuns and missionaries, who had disembarked onto the soil of Viêt-nam. In the distance they could make out Brother Dominic, surrounded by children laughing at his auburn beard and his huge belly; they were pulling his hair. Sister Catherine, too, was surrounded by women much shorter than herself who fingered her golden hair and marveled at her height. Everyone was in good spirits, everyone laughing in the same way at their discoveries. Peace seemed to prevail.

The irrigated plains stretched as far as the eye could see, and their luminous green matched the hard blue sky that would soon turn white. It was early. The heat was overwhelming, the wind had dropped. From the ships, there was nothing to see but those tiny wood and stone houses silhouetted against the horizon. At the edge of the village stood an ochre temple with long curving roofs. The arms of the river vanished into the reeds and the rice-paddies. Huge black buffalos, bent to the ground, were ridden by children wearing straw hats. In his brass spy-glass, the captain made out, far away, green and shadowy mountains lost in the mists. The Viêt-namese were everywhere. On shore, they played in the dinghy left by the missionaries and the nuns. They waved to the sailors.

The soldiers landed in their turn. A little girl, whom Brother Dominic had already taught a few words, shrieked with delight. The children wanted to discover, to learn. But the captain was grim; he approached Brother Dominic. "Brother, it is time to show the power of France."

"Put aside your weapons," the monk replied. "We are here to teach the Gospels. Peace on earth to men of good will. Your muskets are futile, and ugly as well."

An argument ensued; the captain and the Dominican had known each other a long while; they wasted only words. Brother Dominic had no desire for the kind of warfare he had seen in the Americas. He was supported by his men. The captain was alone. The sailors too favored peace.

The heat was unendurable; the sun was to be avoided at all costs. The Viêt-namese offered the missionaries coconut juice, bitter and tepid. They drank it greedily and laughed together, without understanding each other. Brother Dominic proposed to his troupe that they settle in the village: he wanted to remain among the peasants of Viêt-nam. All agreed. The captain allowed them the freedom of their choice and left with his men for Saigon. There were about a hundred of them, armed with blunderbusses and dragging two iron cannons after them. So far from France, authority had disappeared. Interests were different.

Thus ended the first French military expedition to Viêt-nam.

Louis XVI disapproved of this separation. One could not teach the Gospels without weapons or power. He summoned the Primate of the Gauls to Versailles, who listened, stony-faced, to the royal remonstrances without uttering a word. His silence exasperated the King, who suddenly inquired: "What have you to say in your defense?"

The Cardinal knew the difficulties of the realm; he had loved Pierre Pigneau de Bréhaine, his frank asperity, his courage. He answered: "Sire, time passes for men, the Kingdom of God is eternal."

Louis XVI made no reply. In silence, he

stared out at the marble courtyard, the stables with their heavy, disjointed paving-stones, the trees so carefully aligned. Everything was fragile.

The Cardinal withdrew.

Some time later, news came of the death of the captain of the expedition. His men were wounded, slain, or lost in the forests of Viêtnam. It had taken a thousand years for the Viêt-namese to free themselves from the Chinese yoke; against the French, less than two weeks sufficed. These men were brave and armed, but disease seized them. Heat weakened them. They slept in the rice-paddies, tormented by mosquitoes and buffalo-toads whose deafening calls troubled their sleep. They were exhausted and anxious. The silent vegetation was hostile; the water killed them slowly. They grew as filthy and empty as their own wine-casks. The solitude became unendurable. Every morning, they found another man who had been slain in his sleep. Even the gunpowder began to rot, so great was the humidity. The cannons were sinking into the muddy rice-fields. Outside Saigon, peasants armed with pitchforks were waiting for them, an enormous crowd. The French were cruelly massacred. They died alone, far from their country, and far from war.

These peasants who had deposed their Emperor were living in peace.

The soldiers had not sought to understand Viêt-nam: this was not forgiven them.

The monks and nuns began their life in this village, near the rice-paddies. It was called Ba Dien. The Viêt-namese were poor and happy; they grew rice. Sister Catherine never tired of these watery fields and their shifting colors. In the morning, the green sprouts were red with the dawning light; later, the sun gave this flat landscape a singular purity. Under the pitiless sky the women continued planting rice. Finally the day ended, turning the dark-green waters iridescent. How far away France was; and how trifling everything there seemed. In Viêt-nam, among these peasants she understood so poorly, confronting a savage nature, Sister Catherine was humble. Her prayers ascended to the essential, temptations no longer existed. The world was an empty conch.

With the help of the peasant women, the monks constructed a very simple shed, built directly on the ground, without foundations. It was made of bamboo which gave off a dreadful stench, for the wood had been preserved in excrement. Finally Brother Dominic and his men were able to sleep there. It was terribly hot inside, the walls oozed under the noontide sun. But this was the House of God.

The Viêt-namese loved the French. In the beginning, they had found their speech strange, and their height daunting; then they grew accustomed to such things. Friendships developed. The first word Brother Michel learned was *cam on*, which means: thank you.

It was decided to help the Viêt-namese in

their daily tasks. The nuns changed garments, sewed conical hats, and left for the fields. They were exhausted but happy, backs aching, eyes reddened by the brilliance of the day. The Brothers helped the village men; they built dikes, constructed rafts to cross the swollen arms of the Mekong. They knew how to make themselves useful. In the afternoon, when work became impossible, Brother Dominic taught French to anyone who wanted to learn. Only the oldest Viêt-namese man came. He was joined by the men and women who were fond of the monks and nuns. These, in their turn, learned Viêt-namese. It was a difficult language. At last they could speak to one another. The French understood that the war was over.

Nguyen Anh was still in Siam. A new Emperor reigned, supported by the Chinese: peace had returned to Viêt-nam.

After several months, the French had grown accustomed to the climate. They were living in joy. Catechism class had begun, but no one came to it.

One morning, Brother Dominic said Mass under a torrential rain. He stood in the downpour, dressed in white, arms raised to the heavens. The priests sang in Latin; all prayed.

A few days later, the catechism had more success. No one knew why. Perhaps the Viêtnamese liked the nuns' happy smiles.

The missionaries knew each other well. There were five Brothers and three Sisters.

One morning in March 1790, a ship was sighted far offshore, flying the French flag. The landing was summary. News from France was bad: a revolution had begun. Privileges were abolished, the kingdoms of Europe feared still worse. The French realized how alone they were in Viêt-nam: they lived no longer in their country's mind. They said Mass for the King, the Church, and the people of France. Sadness was in their faces. For which some explanation had to be made to the Viêt-namese. That same evening, the villagers invited the French to share their meal. The ship resumed its course toward the Indian seas. Very soon, France once again seemed far away.

The missionaries were active. They had lost their harshness as men and women of the Church. The Sisters had melted the gold of their wedding rings; the Brothers no longer wore crosses. They prayed often, in the evening. And they talked a great deal. Their life was shared, they learned to know one another: they were friends. They slept in one big room, each oblivious of the other's sex. The winter had been cold; it had rained continuously. The mud had invaded their shed. Sister Catherine fell ill; her neck was covered with painful pustules. No one knew what was wrong with her.

The Viêt-namese prepared a poultice. The nun wept, she was afraid to die. Brother Dominic unbuttoned her blue-cotton blouse; for the first time he saw a woman's breasts. They were abundant, white and smooth. The priest placed on her neck a dressing steeped in the juice of certain plants; he waited. Sister Catherine's countenance grew still; her heavy breasts were beaded with sweat. Brother Dominic crossed himself and left the place.

CHAPTER V

The religious community lived like the Viêt-namese, getting up early in the morning before the sun had appeared. They slept on long wooden planks covered with straw matting. The nights were long and cold in winter, scorching in summer. The matting, at first, seemed of an extreme harshness; they had realized its virtues once they had grown accustomed to it. Everyone prayed, then left for their work.

One morning, Brother Dominic met the village elder; leaning on a black-wood cane, he was studying their residence. "What is its name?" he asked in Viêt-namese.

"It has none."

"All our temples have a name."

"Its name is: House of God."

"Every being is a House of God."

The Dominican pondered a moment and said: "Our residence is called: Church of Peace."

The old man produced an inscrutable smile. Satisfied, he hobbled away. Brother Dominic was elated.

The French expedition was intended to help Prince Nguyen Anh to recover his throne; it pleased Brother Dominic that his own Church was the last weapon that remained.

At noon, everyone ate a frugal meal in the fields. They had grown accustomed to the rice wines; the Sisters had suffered some dizziness, but these liquors were invigorating. They dined on their doorstep, sitting on little benches, in the dust of the evening. The sun quickly disappeared, having inflamed the horizon, the orange-tinted sea, the forests. It faded behind the western mountains. The earth was riddled with nocturnal rustlings; the silent paddies reflected the sky. They heard animals in the brush. The heat remained. There were times when everyone feared being unable to breathe; the Dominicans pulled off their harsh cotton shirts. Sweat glistened on their bodies. The Sisters too felt the linen of their dresses sticking to their flesh, which gradually developed rashes.

They never tired of their discovery: Viêt-nam was magnificent. In the beginning they were helped by an old woman. She prepared the meals they all ate together. The missionaries learned how to use chopsticks: *doi dua*. They ate the brown rice in little terra-cotta bowls. On holidays, they discovered other food: caterpillar fritters, orange and crisp. Sister Jeanne picked their white cocoons off the banana palms, then dropped them into tepid brackish water. For Christmas, the old woman made them *tcha ka*; this was a fish from the remote arms of the Mekong; it was simmered in dogfat. Sometimes, they fell sick. Then they were given a thick broth, *pho*. The dense liquid covered a few onion tops, some lotus grains, and raw beef. All of them loved this country.

The Dominicans were lettered. They inclined to writing, and to reading. They avoided each other; Sister Catherine confided her thoughts to the heavy pages of her diary, a kind of long poem: in it she described her new life; the landscapes were especially fine. Even in sickness, she had continued, by the light of a candle, to write about Viêt-nam. How she loved this kind and populous country, with its endless rice-fields! Occasionally she remembered her own country, her own family. She murmured the soldier's prayer: "My Lord, give me the strength to love You." She wrote of their shared life, her admiration for Brother Dominic. Her diary was a retreat in which she chose to sequester herself: only God knew her there.

The winter of 1792 was endless. On Christmas Day, it began to rain. The earth turned to mud. Yet they had to tend to the fields. That evening, they huddled close to the fire. Brother Dominic kept apart; he prized a certain solitude. He was writing long letters on rolls of yellowed paper. They were piled up in a black wooden trunk. The missionary entrusted them to the ships which dropped anchor not far from Saigon. These became increasingly rare. No one would read such long screeds, neither the Prior of Saint-Martin-d'Aubray, to whom Dominic confided the progress of their mission, nor his own family. The cold months dragged on ever more slowly. One evening when Brother Dominic seemed swathed in a remote solitude, Catherine approached him: he was weeping.

To the north, some Jesuits had preached the Gospels in the province of Binh Dinh; they had been massacred, but had left behind a Romanized alphabet which spread rapidly. The Chinese ideograms disappeared: only those on the temple steles remained. At this period, the Catholic community of Ba Dien was one of the most considerable in all Viêt-nam. A large portion of the peasants had converted. Brother

Dominic said Mass every Sunday. The traditions were strong, but he felt God's help in this. Some began teaching the Gospels. Peasants had come from the nearby villages: the French were industrious and smiling.

The missionaries received little news from France. Sometimes a French or foreign priest, a Jesuit, disembarked in Cochin China. He stayed a few days before leaving again for Ceylon or Siam; Viêt-nam was not a welcoming land. The Brothers and Sisters learned in this fashion of the overwhelming events in France. How far away everything seemed to them! Such tidings were scattered reflexions of the past: their world was no longer the same.

They spoke Viêt-namese but remained apart: the differences were so great. In their solitude, they learned to know their own hearts; their desires became less numerous. The agitation of the French cities seemed vain to them, and appearances futile. Without discerning what had changed within themselves, the religious community felt that they were approaching essentials. They had learned detachment, living without unsatisfied hopes. For the first time, they no longer had to kiss the Bishops' heavy rings. The soutanes were dark, and Latin difficult. They taught the prayers in French. They loved God in these humble peasants.

The month of April arrived; the heat grew stifling, once again. Their hands were moist. Every day they had to wash their clothes, which became ever scantier. Finally they slept with scarcely a sheet to cover their bodies because of the humidity of the nights. The women had lost their nuns' broad haunches: field work was arduous. Hidden under her conical hat, her face covered by a veil, like all Viêt-namese women, Sister Jeanne remained extremely pale.

They made expeditions in search of fruit and discovered *long han*, tiny translucent balls

which hung in clusters, the refreshing flesh surrounded by delicate rinds.

The Brothers' faces slowly became emaci-
ated; Brother Dominic lost his paunch and was
obliged to shave his beard: vermin infested it.
Sister Catherine was lovely, the village men
took notice of her body. The old man had said:
"Each being is a House of God." Ailments of
all kinds appeared, which remained without
remedy. Caterpillars fell from the green bamboo and rotted the flesh they crept across. The
monks and nuns learned to take care of themselves. At dawn, they bathed in the tepid waters of the Mekong.

Easter was approaching. They could not
celebrate it: a tornado broke upon them. The
village was devastated; houses were flattened.
The rice-sprouts had been uprooted by the
wind and would have to be replanted. No one
was harmed. The sky had turned an opaque
gray. A silence had come upon everything. Nature seemed to be waiting, anxious. The mis-

sionaries prayed. Only the great trees rustled, then cracked under the sea-winds. The sea roared in the distance. Torrential rains began. Brother Dominic did not celebrate High Mass for Easter; everyone labored in the sheds or in the fields. The Viêt-namese accepted fate with resignation. The French were discovering obedience.

The teaching had to continue. Very soon, Ba Dien was once again a happy village. Brother Dominic decided to leave: Ba Dien was small. The Brothers wanted to remain. They loved Viêt-nam and this peaceful village and feared the obdurate mountains. Long ago, the Dominican had met Pierre Pigneau de Bréhaine: he knew his desires and sought to evangelize more widely. He therefore decided to proceed northwards.

At dawn, when the sky was still blue, he made out the plains which blurred, far away, with the mountains of Annam.

He found a guide who agreed to accompany them. His name was Thach, and he spoke almost no French. The village thanked them. Brother Michel and Sister Catherine would accompany Brother Dominic: they would take with them their Bible and a few books, their back-packs, some victuals.

They left in the morning.

CHAPTER VI

The French religious community of Viêt-nam never learned of the death of King Louis XVI. They had learned of France's perilous situation from ships which put into Saigon. After Christmas 1792, there were no more of these: the nations of Europe were caught up in torment. At the beginning, the Brothers and Sisters were anxious. Not knowing was worst of all. They could not imagine the situation of their country. By Christmas 1793, no ship had anchored at Saigon for a year: they understood that they had been forgotten.

In France, chaos reigned after 1791; the

King had been arrested at Varennes, disguised as a bourgeois. Paris had chosen a National Guard, a mayor. The clergy, itself, was divided. Everywhere the press grew stronger. People read aloud *L'ami du Peuple* in the streets of Paris. Important reforms were put into effect; regional dialects were beginning to disappear, and the metric system was born.

Viêt-nam was living in calm and oblivion; France in uncertainty. The government was weak: everyone hoped for war. The Girondists sought to spread the Revolution; the King hoped for a victory of foreign princes. Coalitions were formed. France declared war on the Kingdom of Hungary; Rouget de l'Isle wrote his war-song for the Armies of the Rhine, which inflamed all hearts. In August 1792, Paris rose up: Louis XVI was deposed. The Convention had just appeared. The years changed, the seasons flourished: this was Year I of the Republic.

The Committee of Public Safety instituted a reign of terror. Louis XVI was beheaded; the guillotine operated ceaselessly. Foreign coalitions were repulsed: the Battle of Valmy was won.

In the west of France, a mass uprising of three hundred thousand men was decided upon. The Catholic religion began to be persecuted. Priests were hunted, monks and nuns expelled: they were suspected of collusion with the enemy. Parish registers were burned; they were replaced by the thick volumes of the *état civil*. Works of sacred art were destroyed; for a while, the Goddess Reason was worshipped. Churches became haunts of pleasure. Vast orgies were held in them; naked women were seen yielding to the desires of several men, on the altars of the Lord. In March 1793, weary of blasphemies and suffering, the Vendée rebelled. Republican troops were anything but numerous there, and poorly organized: they were defeated. The Royal and Catholic army seized Angers, but was defeated outside of Nantes. Young General Hoche was chosen to organize the repression: the winter of 1794 was terrible.

The benefactors who had sponsored Pierre Pigneau de Bréhaine's expedition were rich men. They left France for the neighboring monarchies; some were murdered, and their goods confiscated. The clergy was dismembered; hierarchies had disappeared, memories blurred. A hundred fifty thousand écus had been expended without security: no one took responsibility for that. Chaos reigned; lines of communication were cut. The Atlantic ports were blockaded by the Royal British Navy. On the docks of La Rochelle, the rigging lay pathetically coiled. Each man machinated his own survival. Those who knew, no longer thought of Viêt-nam, or were eager to forget: the monks of Cochin China were privateers.

CHAPTER VII

Saint-Martin-d'Aubray was a Vendéan abbey; a few windswept houses of gray stone adjoined the great barn of a church, a low, dark eleventh-century structure with a cloister on one side. The cloister itself was cold and empty, but around it were a series of tiny rooms, sealed by oak doors on heavy hinges. Few monks lived at Saint-Martin-d'Aubray; a dozen, at most. The Abbot was an old man who could no longer see; it was necessary to read to him what he could not imagine. A few young Brothers assisted him, eager and learned. The abbeys of France lived by the harvest of their fields; some produced honey, others brandy.

But Saint-Martin was swept by the salt winds of the Atlantic. The fields were a wild heathland, reached by a long path of pale earth, stewn with sky-blue pebbles. A Calvary dominated these fallow plains: here time had come to a stop. Yet Saint-Martin navigated in spirit beyond the seas; by day, the Brothers labored over heavy tomes. After vespers, they dreamed, around the fire, of unknown lands. The abbey preserved the secrets of the Dominicans. Their expeditions were recorded, as well as the funds pledged. The Church thereby knew where its missionaries were preaching, as well as their number, and the progress of their missions. This was a wearisome task, one propitious to dreaming.

Some missions were of importance. That of Pierre Pigneau de Bréhaine less so. Little attention was paid to it. Items of information were contradictory: a Mass had been said at Versailles for the vanished religious community. They had disembarked at Viêt-nam some time afterwards. The Dominicans themselves no longer knew the number of their missionaries in the lands of the East. Since 1792, Saint-Martin no longer recorded the progress of their evangelization.

Over the years, a correspondence had been established beyond the seas. The missionaries wrote to their order. Exotic letters arrived from Brazil, from Ceylon, from the Americas. Those from Viêt-nam were rare. The writings of Brother Dominic had rotted in the humidity of the voyage. The priests and nuns were soon forgotten in the prayers of the order; their existence was epitomized in a few letters.

In June 1793, the National Guard presented itself at the abbey; the soldiers attempted to seize the Dominican archives. The oaken doors remained closed. The commander was sent for; eventually he arrived and sought to negotiate.

The peasants left the neighboring fields armed with their pitchforks. Fighting broke out; blunderbusses were fired. The monks prayed in the cloister. The soldiers finally entered, bearing huge resin torches. The doors of the archival chambers were forced, and the heavy leather ledgers set on fire. Wind fanned the flames: the blaze lasted all night. The white flames rose into the sky, like a beacon. In silence the monks watched the fire turn to embers and thought of their brothers at the other end of the earth. They were alone.

All that summer, events of this kind occurred. At Saint-Martin, years of correspondence and of archives had vanished.

Early in the morning, the peasants and their wives came to help the Brothers; they attempted to save some of the ledgers. Almost nothing was left. The huge building had collapsed; only the old stones of the cloister were still standing. A column of black smoke rose from them. Some of the abbey's records were saved. The pages of the ledgers were blackened or burned: they were illegible. So it was that on a cold and hate-filled night in the Vendée, the Church definitively forgot the French monks and nuns who were evangelizing Viêt-nam.

The Province of Binh Tri Thien fell in 1800. Prince Nguyen Anh seized the imperial fortress of Hué the same year and reigned once more over Viêt-nam. After several years of exile, he had returned to his country. He invented tortures of a new refinement. On some mornings, bodies were found near Saigon, hacked to pieces; they had no faces. The Prince had armed his partisans. His heart was bitter; his son had died at the other end of the world, far from his own people and from his country. France had abandoned him. He regretted having lowered himself to ask for that country's help. He had permitted missionaries to preach their Gospel in his country. Now Nguyen Anh had again seen the rice-fields glittering between the arms of the Mekong; he had wept and thought of his ancestors.

Nguyen Anh learned of the Dominicans' life at Ba Dien; he believed the community to be important, he sought revenge. He set out with his men; in Saigon such an expedition caused astonishment. Eventually they reached Ba Dien; the peasants were in the rice-fields. Those who were not, fled: they could do nothing more. That morning, the Dominicans were praying and reading the Gospels. All were massacred, Sister Jeanne was raped. Nguyen Anh did not bother to burn their books, and the peasants took possession of them. The bodies were thrown into a ditch; it was filled in the next day. The Church of Peace was razed; Nguyen Anh was surprised at the small number of missionaries. He had admired the gold hair of the woman his men had taken with such violence.

A few days before, Sister Catherine, Brother Dominic, and Brother Michel had left for the center of the country: Annam.

CHAPTER VIII

They crossed the Mekong on a wooden ferry; the boat was flat and square. A man steered it with a long pole which he thrust into the shivering water. This arm of the Mekong was muddy. The three Dominicans saw the north shore gradually approach, covered with reeds and scrub. The water was red, without eddies; the white sky blinded them.

They had arrived with other peasants; some were taking their buffalo across the river; children were playing on their mother's backs. Sister Catherine, Brother Michel, and Brother Dominic had waited in the dazzling sunlight. The crossing lasted only a few minutes: it felt like eternity. The southern shore receded, with all its rustling life; the northern shore seemed calm. Nothing stirred.

All that day they walked in silence. The two monks and the nun followed their impassive guide who breathed slowly. Each was deep in thought. At first, they were overcome by sadness: they had lived a long time with those who remained at Ba Dien. They had discovered Viêt-nam together. Then exhaustion stripped them of all thought. Thach occasionally pointed out a stele of the Ngo Dynasty, engraved with ancient ideograms. Some were carved with flourishes which were the signs of sky and earth. In the forests they discovered heavy stones, worn by humidity, captives of the lianas. With difficulty they could decipher the adages on them. Brother Dominic loved these harmonies of man and matter.

He dreamed on, endlessly; everything seemed easy to him. The Viêt-namese of Ba Dien had joyfully acepted Christianity and its message of peace. But they had not ceased venerating the Tortoise, the Unicorn, and the Dragon. The Phoenix, symbol of immortality and grace, was celebrated according to the lunar months. The ancestors were worshipped on each hearth. Sixty days after the Spring Festival, the Night of Perfect Clarity was still celebrated: the dead and the living met each other then as the night the day. Brother Dominic doubted: the peasants listened to the Gospels; they continued to believe in their ancient gods. Viêt-nam preserved everything, and everything mingled here within eternity. Beings passed, like the wind over the rice-fields. The rice-sprouts showed their joyous green.

The landscape had changed. The forests were sealed by their interlacing lianas, covered with mysterious leaves; the ground was marshy. They walked in tepid, smelly water, braided with long hidden roots; after crossing the Mekong, the rice-fields had vanished into wild vegetation. Thach never lost his way in the green thickets; the dense textures were always identical. The network of lianas and banyans was endless, and caused an infinite lassitude. The sun barely penetrated the flat foliage of the great trees, but generated a heavy moisture there, comparable to that of the Orangeries of Versailles which Sister Catherine had visited long ago.

A few days had been enough to exhaust them. They had left thoughts and prayers behind; they were trying not to stumble. The forest encircled them with its murmurs: a secret fauna lived here. Huge serpents slid off the bamboos; buffalo-toads croaked in the distance. One evening, after walking twenty days, they saw stars in the sky once again.

Brother Michel fell ill. No one knew what was the matter. The guide prepared remedies from plants. Nothing availed. He folded his arms and began to wait. The missionary was not suffering: he could no longer walk. His legs were paralyzed by a mysterious weakness. They laid him out, limb by limb. All day, Catherine and Dominic wiped his face. Brother Michel had incessant fevers. He was burning. After dark he spoke endlessly, and forgot. Sometimes he was lucid and recognized his companions; together, they prayed. He seemed lost in a solitude from which nothing could release him. Thach told them that Brother Michel was doomed; he had recognized the marsh fever. After the fourth seizure, Brother Michel stopped breathing: their prayers were bitter.

In the morning, they set out. The orange plains were calm. The moments passed slowly. A light breeze, almost cool, flecked the banana palms. They found fruits; Thach filled his net bag with *long han*. Brother Dominic, sitting on a stone, read the Bible. The moist pages had faded, then stuck together. He recited a verse aloud, then broke off: to the north appeared the dark mountain slopes, suddenly revealed by the mists. Sister Catherine looked too: she was smiling. They were eager to arrive, to find coolness and straw matting.

They never mentioned Brother Michel. Both knew the diseases which lay in wait for them. They spoke of other things. As they drew closer to the mountains, the humidity lessened.

"Dominic, do you believe we truly converted the peasants of Ba Dien?"

"I've thought about it for a long time, Catherine. They loved God in our work in the fields, in your smiles. I don't know if they loved only Him."

Thach walked ahead of them; Brother Dominic spoke of his past. Catherine listened to him all day long.

They had grown thin. Exhaustion was evident in their faces. In September 1793, the guide showed them a circular barrier of boulders. This was the ancient volcano T'nung, inside which lay an emerald lake. The water was cold, pure. They rested here for several days. After dark the smooth peaks were silhouetted against the sky like dreams; the full moon smoothed the water of the lake. The silence was almost disquieting. Thach slept; Dominic grew worried about Catherine, who had left them for a moment and had not returned. He stood up and followed the path of black stones she had taken. He walked a few minutes, and the inner slopes of the volcano became less steep. The water seemed shallower; he saw Catherine naked. Her clothes were folded on a lump of dry lava. Catherine was standing in the water up to her knees, making her way into the impassive lake in which her body was reflected, a white oblong. She crouched slowly, then stood up again, wet now. She seemed far away as she advanced into the lake. Dominic made out the contours of her flesh extended by the night. She was delicate; she seemed happy in the cold waters of the volcano. Suddenly he thought she had vanished: she had stretched out, as though dissolved into the sky's reflections. Dominic walked back along the stony path.

They left T'nung; a few yards to the north began Giai Lai Kon Tum, the Great Plateau.

Dominic had left France at the age of thirty-one. He had gone to the Americas. War reigned there, he mentioned it rarely. He still remembered the long passage over the Sargasso Sea; their ships could not find an anchorage. Each was left on its own. Of the Americas, he remembered white landscapes; in winter, it had snowed several days at a time. He still dreamed of that cold. The religious communities were numerous: he set out for the French provinces. Québec was enveloped in melancholy auburn tints. He had taught the catechism there for two years: he felt he was of little use. He had returned to France. At La Rochelle, he was told that Pierre Pigneau de Bréhaine was preparing an expedition for Cochin China: he embarked.

They entered Cong Rai, a village of huts roofed with mud and branches. In summer, these structures collapsed under torrential rains. Here Dominic decided to stop at last. He thanked Thach, who set out once again for Cochin China. The peasants of the village welcomed the monk and the nun with respect, for they spoke Viêt-namese. They themselves did not understand this language.

Evening fell, they slept in a hut at the entrance to the village, redolent of green rice and lotus seeds. Dominic and Catherine discovered a new life; the village was arranged around one particular hut. The women dressed differently and wore a dark bandeau around their hair. Many smoked long white pipes. Their gowns were long and black; Catherine wore one too, in order to combat the cold. Winter was approaching; Dominic worked with the Gia-rai. He helped them cultivate beans, feed hogs. In the morning mists, he shouted commands to the elephant that was uprooting tree-stumps. The wind got in everywhere. In the hut they were assigned, the fire burned all day long. They were living better than at Ba Dien. Dominic hunted wild boar with the peasants. But their solitude was great. Once again, they had to learn everything; the language was more complex than Viêt-namese. The accentuations required a different syntax. The mountain people received them kindly, but they were hard workers and left the missionaries to themselves.

Evenings, Dominic and Catherine rarely prayed; they needed to talk. They described France to each other, their life, their memories. Dominic had brought a few books; he read aloud the sonnets of Petrarch and Homer's *Iliad*. The days extended into the cold of winter. In January, it began to rain. A fine drizzle took possession of the plateau: it seemed never to stop. White clouds severed the nearby mountains from their base. The humidity conquered everything; it steeped their bodies in solitude.

CHAPTER IX

The winter lasted months and months. Only in May did the sun appear. The low clouds dissolved. The sky turned blue and began to embrace the earth. The mountains were splendid; the heat was less trying than at Saigon. The air was swept by breezes. Tornados never came to Annam; they broke up on the mountains, frayed out into winds that were engulfed in the cols and valleys. Then the sky darkened; the desolation was tremendous. There were fewer peasants, isolated in their villages of huts. At the approach of the great rains, the dark-green slopes were alarming:

everyone took refuge at the edge of the forests or in the mud and straw sheds.

Spring, then summer happened. The new seasons brought joy to Catherine and Dominic. Nature was so intensely alive; the valleys turned into fantastic landscapes inhabited by elephants and towering plants. The light of life had returned.

Sister Catherine was still young. She had been born near Bordeaux, in 1760. She had kept the love of the ochre stones, the open spaces, the sun. She remained pale. At twenty, she entered the convent. Not by constraint: she had the vocation. She knew how to bring relief to souls, solicitude to bodies. Catherine walked for several years beneath the shadows of the cloister, then grew weary of closed spaces. The sisters seemed dry and melancholy; she left. No one had much use for a woman missionary; her milky complexion betrayed her fragility. Pierre Pigneau de Bréhaine received and accepted her: she had a strong character, though timid. The presence of women would surely reassure the Viêt-namese. She sailed on the *Saint-Paul*; she was pure and deliberate, for all her dreaminess. Her life was secret, her devotion silent. With Dominic, too, she listened a great deal. She loved his warmth, his enthusiasm. Her faith was humble.

The months passed, then the years.

It was a rough, austere life they led. They prayed, evenings, before the candle flame. Their hearts were no longer in it. Their psalms were merely habit. Their hopes had grown faint in the languors of Viêt-nam. The difficulties, the death of Brother Michel, weighed upon them. Every religious feeling seemed remote, ultimately outside of themselves. Dominic and Catherine knew they had been forgotten by the world; they judged their presence to be futile. The peasants listened to them and smiled, but the holy words were lost in the echoes of the mountains. They were overwhelmed by an inner emptiness: they were alone, and weary.

The Gia-rai believed in a world inhabited by invisible spirits. God was in each thing. Every being, however inanimate, bore a soul. These Viêt-namese were docile and tranquil. Patient, they venerated the universe in each of its signs. The rain spoke to them, as did the moon and the wind. The missionaries offered them a book animated by remote legends; they were diverting. But the gods of earth and sky were incredible and close at hand: they made each leaf tremble. Certain summer nights when signs were revealed, the village rustled with happy moans. Man and woman were in accord with the universe.

The news spread that Nguyen Anh was once again Emperor of Viêt-nam. Tonkin and Cochin China belonged to him. His reigning years were severe. Order was imposed. He assumed the name Gia Long and began to reform the country. He established a Manchu penal code; he built palaces, founded schools. Dominic and Catherine also learned of the fate of their companions in Saigon. They heard of the horrible death of Sister Jeanne, raped and then strangled. Sadness was upon them. They had known these friends in the faith; the expedition of Pierre Pigneau de Bréhaine was over. Only the two missionaries in Annam remained, forgotten by the world and forgetting themselves. The meaning of their presence in Viêt-nam had drowned in the dramas, the seasons. But they were captives of this country.

Yet both experienced the joy of their free and simple lives. Their souls were laid bare: the essential remained. Their labors were healthy. They fed the hogs, the dry and skinny fowls. Catherine had learned to ride the elephant that uprooted tree-stumps between the narrow valleys. They discovered the rhinoceros, and tigers with virgin fangs. Evenings, by the fire, they joined the peasants in summoning the souls of fire and of water. The songs were shrill and brief. The women danced, dressed in black robes. The two missionaries discovered the lives of others: they learned about their own. They were shown certain pale-wood sculptures which represented the spirits of the forests.

They spoke of their country. What had become of France? They knew nothing. Versailles had lost its truth; in their minds, Ceylon and its low, bright-colored houses was closer. Their families were living in a strange and somehow vanished world. Catherine let her youth speak for her. She told Dominic of her vocation, the coldness of the tiles on which she had prostrated herself, arms outstretched. She had betrothed herself to God. She told him also of the rigors of the voyage, the sailors who spied on her, the impenetrable murmurs of the night. She had been overcome by the novelty of things. Gradually, her religious convictions had eroded. She was not anxious; she was surprised. The years had passed. Her faith had been effaced, and had left only the psalms and her joy. They were leading a life of purity in the high mountains of Annam. Dominic and Catherine no longer desired to return to France.

For several days, they had made their way toward the mountains, accompanied by an old peasant. He walked slowly. The monk and the nun discovered unimaginable landscapes. On the southern slopes, there were strange rice-fields, tiny ponds sealed with low walls. The rice-sprouts spread over these terraces like geological lines left by the ages. Man seemed absent. Sometimes they glimpsed a woman planting sprouts who vanished then among those canals. The valleys unfolded endlessly before their eyes. The old peasant spoke Viêt-namese; they told him about France; he understood.

"Our friends have forgotten us, old man, and God speaks to us so little."

He had answered: "How green the rice-fields are; they are the mirror of heaven."

They bathed in the waters of a spring which leaped ice-cold from the rocks. It was a diversion, a refreshment. They angled for bright-colored fish with unknown names.

Dominic and Catherine attended the village festivities. They began to understand their meaning. Certain days were dedicated to the young women, who exchanged bronze bracelets with the men who pleased them. By evening, the elders listened to the young women's dreams and predicted each couple's future. Sometimes the auguries were grim, or vague. Then the preparations ceased. Otherwise the young bride was welcomed into her new family, perfumed with all the savors of the forest, dressed in black silk. The entire village shared a grand banquet of sticky rice and soy sprouts steeped in bitter sauces.

One morning Catherine remembered the soldier's prayer: "Lord, grant me the strength to love You."

She had that strength no longer. Her faith had slowly disintegrated. They never taught the catechism as they had done not far from Saigon.

CHAPTER X

With the summer's end came the rainy season. Dominic painted on long silk scrolls the Malay junks that had been pointed out to him. Catherine had long since stopped writing: she read Petrarch.

The huts were made of mud and straw, baked hard by the sun. Under the endless rain, the roofs began to cave in. Thick layers of earth flaked off. Then the whole roof slid loose in viscous pieces. The village roofs of Annam dissolved into dark water. Dominic and Catherine waited in their hut, leaning over a few embers. They were silent. Their faces were attentive; they listened to branches breaking and the wind whistling through the rocks. The sky was tormented. Their one candle went out. The rain did not relent for two days. All they could hear was the rustling of the forest leaves.

The village was deserted: the peasants had withdrawn into their huts. The rain pelted the rice-terraces on the mountainsides. The green sprouts yielded, beaten into the overflowing mud. The streaming water carried away the soil. Everyone waited patiently, obediently; in their hut, Dominic and Catherine saw their hair grow wringing wet. The rain was penetrating the layers of straw; a smell of fermentation spread around them. Their faces darkened with the black and humid dust that fell from the ceiling. Catherine's blond hair had thickened into dark clots. Their garments were sopping too; Dominic was half-naked. Their skin was wet and red with cold and rashes; Catherine was wearing a gray cotton dress which clung to her body. Her hardened breasts were modelled by the rough cloth.

The silence triumphed. They did not speak;

they watched one another, hoping the rains would stop. Their clothes bothered them. Catherine was trembling: her lips were white. Spasms convulsed her body. Dominic was alarmed; he hugged her against him. He smelled her warm breath, the thinness of her skin, and of her dress. He rubbed his hand against her back, against the nape of her neck.

Then he caressed her. She said nothing; she waited. The day passed in silence. Only the monk's hand which covered Catherine's body spoke. His eyes were hard, his loins still hidden. Dominic had discovered her breasts; they were white and grainy with cold. He warmed her slowly with the same sweetness he found in her. New landscapes were opening for them; Dominic was discovering its geography. She could feel, now, its profundity. Each of her pores oozed salty water, blackened by earth. Their hands were withered with moisture. Their breathing guided their discoveries. The universe appeared to them.

The rains did not stop. Day was no different from night. They ate little, only a few fruits. Slowly, Catherine stretched out on her matting. She kept her eyes open. The winds blew. Dominic opened her dress and exposed her body: it was white, as luminous as whatever daylight there was. The monk stared endlessly at the pale flesh. He seemed to find new colors in it. His hands grazed each particle of these lands. Catherine had opened her arms, forming a cross. Dominic caressed her delicate thighs, her hollow belly. The nun yielded to the sensations that passed over her, through her. She was attentive.

The rain was not so heavy; at last they emerged from the hut. The village was dark, even grim. No one had left his dwelling. They looked up and observed the clouds in pursuit. The night was on the move. The stars had vanished; the forests, on the mountainside, seemed to brace themselves and rise. The huts dissolved in the torrent. Nature was making approximate, unfinished gestures. The wind caressed each being, revealing its every sensation. All things discovered themselves; the spirits, in them, awakened. Dominic became the tiger crouching, wet through, under the banana palms. The elephant loomed nearby. Life was close; the night remained.

He saw her naked: she withstood his elated gaze. Catherine smiled. He parted her legs and caressed her belly gently. Her hair had grown darker, waiting under the rain. She breathed gently. He spoke no word, he did not kiss her. He could not have enough of her body. Everything, around them, vanished. With his hands he explored this varying landscape; his own nipples reddened at their hardened tips. A faint down shadowed her parted thighs. He knew his desire was strong. He entered her, beneath the straw roof from which the earth, dissolved, kept dripping.

CHAPTER XI

Dominic forgot himself in her. Catherine yielded beneath his body which had taken her so far. The ground beneath them had turned to mud. Her hands held Dominic close. She breathed noiselessly, faster. Their darkened eyes were fixed upon the depths of life. They plunged into each other. They did not fall asleep; when the murmurs of the earth replaced their breath, they lay and watched the sky. Their thoughts escaped. They had chosen their oblivion and in it found themselves infinitely present.

The village elder, in his clumsy canvas trousers, invoked the spirit of the rains. Hands raised to the sky, he chattered endlessly. The mountains continued to flow into mud.

The rain lasted three days more. Dominic and Catherine continued to discover each other. He would caress the nape of her neck, opening his eyes to stare at her; each felt the other's desire. They spoke little. The signs of sky and earth instructed them. They loved the certain presence of their bodies: they were protected by the universe. The lunar reflections of T'nung were clear now. Catherine's body had lost its fluidity: it was real.

Six years later, Catherine and Dominic died. How much life they had known! The Viêtnamese mourned, for they had loved them. Like Sister Armande, Catherine had suffered an unslakable thirst. Dominic lived so close to her that he contracted her illness. He did not want to remain alone. The two of them perished in peace; they were happy. The Gia-rai buried their bodies at the outskirts of the village. As the monk and the nun had requested, they planted a bamboo cross on which was cut, in Viêt-namese:

For our God and for France

Catherine and Dominic loved their freedom. They had not forgotten their country. So ended the French expedition to Viêt-nam. Of the crews who embarked on the *Saint-Jean* and the *Saint-Paul*, no survivor remained. Viêt-nam had regained peace; very few Catholics were in the country. Saigon prospered, gradually influenced by Ceylon. Annam was inhabited by mountain people oblivious of the world.

CHAPTER XII

In 1820, Minh Mang, a Confucian whose education had been entirely Chinese, closed his country to external influences. France, however, sent other expeditions; important ones. Algeria had been conquered; Indochina would be. Later, Angkor Wat and its enormous stones interwoven by lianas became French; Catholicism was forgotten. The soldiers were merciless. In Saigon they found some signs of the Dominicans' former presence. That was all; Pierre Pigneau de Bréhaine was forgotten, as well as the boy emperor Canh.

In 1856, the remote villages of Annam were explored. Nothing had changed. Elephants continued to uproot the tree-stumps; the roofs of the huts continued to dissolve under the rains each autumn. The French expeditionary forces discovered the bamboo cross in the village where Brother Dominic and Sister Catherine had lived. This unique cross provoked a certain astonishment. Indeed their life in such a place seemed incredible. The chaplain had his doubts: he broke the cross. Forgetting was the order of the day.

Dominic and Catherine had escaped the persecution organized by Nguyen Anh. Towards the end of his reign he pursued the minorities inhabiting the high plateaux, overly independent for his taste.

One summer night in 1802, armed men entered Cong Rai; they were looking for two white missionaries. They searched the dwellings one by one. They were amazed to find no occidental clue. At last they pushed open the door of the hut where Dominic and Catherine lay sleeping, naked, in each other's arms. The man had rested one hand on the young woman's breast. Her belly was moist with sweat and with semen. They had made love. A deep silence remained. The soldiers wondered. They expected to find men and women with hard eyes and hostile words, who did not partake of each other's bodies. The tranquility moved the soldiers, as did the pallor of the monk and the nun.

Without a gesture, they left for other villages.